Adventure SPORTS

CAVING

Stephanie Turnbull

A+
Smart Apple Media

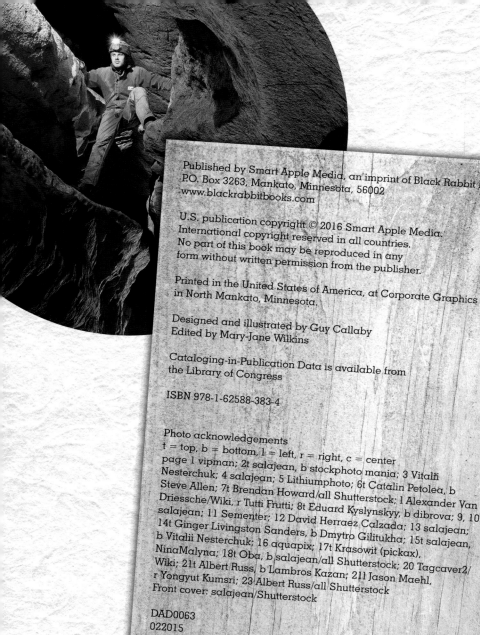

Published by Smart Apple Media, an imprint of Black Rabbit Books
P.O. Box 3263, Mankato, Minnesota, 56002
www.blackrabbitbooks.com

Printed in the United States of America, at Corporate Graphics
in North Mankato, Minnesota.

Designed and illustrated by Guy Callaby
Edited by Mary-Jane Wilkins

Cataloging-in-Publication Data is available from
the Library of Congress

ISBN 978-1-62588-383-4

Photo acknowledgements
t = top, b = bottom, l = left, r = right, c = center
page 1 vipman; 2t salajean, b stockphoto mania; 3 Vitalii
Nesterchuk; 4 salajean; 5 Lithiumphoto; 6t Catalin Petolea, b
Steve Allen; 7t Brendan Howard/all Shutterstock; l Alexander Van
Driessche/Wiki, r Tutti Frutti; 8t Eduard Kyslynskyy, b dibrova; 9, 10
salajean; 11 Sementer; 12 David Herraez Calzada; 13 salajean;
14t Ginger Livingston Sanders, b Dmytro Gilitukha; 15t salajean,
b Vitalii Nesterchuk; 16 aquapix; 17t Krasowit (pickax),
NinaMalyna; 18t Oba, b salajean/all Shutterstock; 20 Tagcaver2/
Wiki; 21t Albert Russ, b Lambros Kazan; 21l Jason Maehl,
r Yongyut Kumsri; 23 Albert Russ/all Shutterstock
Front cover: salajean/Shutterstock

DAD0063
022015
9 8 7 6 5 4 3 2 1

CONTENTS

Feel the thrill   4

Amazing caves   6

Get the gear   8

The right ropes   10

Start training   12

Cave grades   14

Extreme caving   16

Smart planning   18

Emergency!   20

Glossary   22

Websites   23

Index   24

FEEL THE THRILL

Think you have the skill, strength, and stamina to try caving? If you like the idea of venturing into weird and wonderful underground worlds, read on...

Making your way through narrow cave passages takes skill, energy, and good balance!

Take the challenge

Imagine lowering yourself into the depths of a mysterious **chasm**, scrambling over rocks, squeezing through passages with only a torch to light your way, then emerging into an echoing chamber where no one has ever set foot. Caving is an extreme adventure!

4

Tough stuff

Caving can be dangerous, so don't attempt it without the right equipment, skills, and training. You must be physically fit to climb, **rappel**, crawl, and even swim—and mentally prepared to think quickly and calmly in life-or-death situations.

THRILL SEEKER

Edouard-Alfred Martel (France)

FEAT
One of the first cavers. Survived landslides and floods to explore caves all over the world.

WHERE AND WHEN
France, Ireland, England, Mallorca, 1888-1914

EXTREME BUT TRUE The Son Doong Cave in Vietnam is the world's largest cave. One chamber is 3 miles (5 km) long and 656 feet (200m) high. It even has a jungle growing inside it!

Caves can be treacherous places. Always plan and prepare well before heading underground.

AMAZING CAVES

Caves range from small hollows in cliffs to complex tunnel systems winding miles below ground. Where do you want to explore?

Cave types

Caves are formed by waves crashing against cliffs, or underground rivers carving out tunnels and chambers in **limestone**. Some hold lakes, while others are dry. There are even ice caves in **glaciers**.

This huge cave is high in the mountains of Romania.

The rocky coastline of Malta has many natural arches and sea caves.

Stunning sights

Rock **minerals** and water combine to create amazing underground features. There are towering **stalagmites**, hanging **stalactites**, and cave pearls formed from sand grains and minerals.

There are also beautiful frozen waterfalls of minerals called flowstones. These are formed by water flowing over rock, leaving deposits that build up into smooth, curved layers.

Minerals in dripping water create strange shapes over years.

EXTREME BUT TRUE The longest cave system in the world is the Mammoth Cave in Kentucky. It stretches an incredible 390 miles (628 km).

Fantastic formations of cave crystals (above left) and stalagmites (above) are often lit up and displayed in impressive tourist caves.

GET THE GEAR

If you're heading off caving, you need the right gear. The ground will be uneven, rocks can be slippery, and the temperature may plunge. And of course it will be dark!

Dress well

You need tough, hard-wearing clothes for squeezing past jagged rocks, slithering over rubble, or squelching through muddy tunnels. You may need thermal layers underneath to keep warm, and waterproof layers on top to stay dry.

Caving can damage your clothes, so wear things you don't mind ruining!

EXTREME BUT TRUE

Some caves are totally underwater and can only be explored in a wetsuit and diving gear!

Have a hat

A good helmet is essential. It could save your life in a rock fall or other accident. Wear a helmet with a head lamp attached, so you can keep your hands free—and take a spare lamp, just in case.

Be prepared

Gloves protect your hands as you scramble over rocks, while knee and elbow pads are useful when crawling through narrow spaces. Footwear should be strong and sturdy, with good grips.

THE RIGHT ROPES

Going underground usually involves using ropes, harnesses, and other special climbing equipment to lower yourself down steep drops.

Rappeling gear

Climbing rope is smooth, strong, and slightly stretchy. You clip it to your harness and anchor it to rocks, then slide down. Special devices let you control your speed and stop safely. Always go caving with a friend to hold the rope steady.

EXTREME BUT TRUE The world's steepest vertical cave **shaft** is in Vrtoglavica Cave in Slovenia. The sheer drop is a dizzying 1,978 feet (603m).

Rappeling is the only way to get into very steep caves. Move steadily and smoothly, paying attention to the rock around you.

Caving knots

It's vital to attach your rope securely to your harness. Here's how to do it.

1. Tie a figure of eight about 3 feet (1m) from one end of the rope.

2. Thread the end of the rope through your harness.

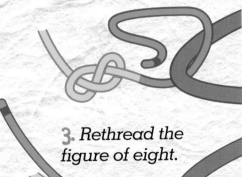

3. Rethread the figure of eight.

4. Tie the end to the main piece of rope to stop it from coming undone.

It's essential to wear a harness, helmet, rappeling device, and safety gear to descend sheer rock faces.

THRILL SEEKER

Sean Rovito (Mexico)

FEAT
Rappeled into caves in Mexico and discovered a rare salamander believed extinct

WHERE AND WHEN
Honduras, 2010

START TRAINING

As well as being able to climb and rappel, you must learn to recognize different cave features and dangers. Join a caving club and build up your skills gradually.

Caving experts will teach you how to stay safe and enjoy your caving adventures!

EXTREME BUT TRUE Cavers who have spent days in caves often feel strangely tired when they come out, as well as extremely sensitive to light, sound, and temperature.

Up and down

Learn how to climb and rappel with an expert who will watch you closely and give you help. Start with very short drops of 33 to 49 feet (10 to 15m) and never try anything you're unsure about.

Cave comfort

Going deep underground can be a scary, **claustrophobic** experience. Start with straightforward caves where you don't need to climb, then move on to trickier tunnels. Always go with experienced adults.

Keep calm in tight spots. Use your lamp to look for wider sections.

CAVE GRADES

Caves are divided into five grades of difficulty, so you know how challenging each will be. Pick grades to suit your skills and never attempt anything too dangerous!

Grade 1 Very easy: You need a helmet and torch, and can walk through passages.

Grade 1 caves are often open to tourists and sightseeing groups.

Grade 2 Easy: A few more obstacles, but fine for beginners.

Some caves have a few big rocks to scramble down.

Grade 3 Fairly hard: Some difficult sections, so you need good caving skills.

Grade 4 Hard: Caves have big drops, underground water, very narrow passages, and other hazards. Take climbing equipment and emergency gear.

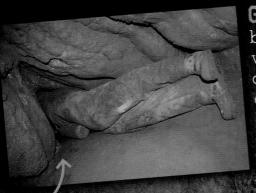

You'll need to crawl and wriggle through narrow passages. They're not for beginners!

The deepest, darkest caves take skill and nerve to get through safely.

Grade 5 Extremely hard: Many hazards and the route may be hard to follow. You need experience, technical knowledge, special gear, and a guide.

EXTREME BUT TRUE High-grade caves may have chimneys. These are very tight vertical slots that you climb by pushing your feet and hands against the sides and heaving yourself up.

EXTREME CAVING

Some caving experts take huge risks in the quest for ever more thrilling underground adventures.

Cave diving

Cave divers love to plunge into the inky depths of underground rivers and lakes in search of marvelous sights. There's a high risk of being trapped against rocks or swept away in strong **currents**—and if their torch fails, they won't have a clue where they're going.

Explorers may use rock-clearing tools to open up new passageways or find a way into chambers.

Cave digging

Some cave explorers clear ways through rock using tools and sometimes even explosives. It's extremely risky and can lead to rock falls, which could trap or crush cavers.

180 ft
350 ft
520 ft
690 ft
860 ft
1,030 ft
1,200 ft

Cave

Chrysler Building

EXTREME BUT TRUE

The Cave of Swallows in Mexico is so deep you could stand a skyscraper as tall as New York's Chrysler Building inside. Some crazy cavers jump into it wearing parachutes, which they open in the 12 seconds before they hit the ground.

SMART PLANNING

Plan and prepare well before you go caving to prevent problems and make sure your adventure doesn't turn to disaster.

Caving checklist

Here are some essentials to consider when planning a caving expedition.

What kind of cave is it?

Check the cave grade (see pages 14-15) and any hazards, such as rivers or steep drops. Have the right gear, such as climbing equipment; make sure you know how to use it.

*Make sure you have good-quality rope and **carabiners** to secure it.*

Underground water may be deep and flow fast, so watch your step.

Will it be cold or wet?

If so, you need warm, waterproof clothing and spare layers in case you get wet. Duct tape is useful for patching up clothes that snag and rip against jagged rocks.

What's the weather like? The weather above ground can affect your trip more than you realize, as heavy rain can quickly flood tunnels. Check the weather forecast carefully. If in doubt, don't go.

Survival kit

Take a small rucksack containing supplies such as food, drink, a spare lamp, and a pocket knife. Pack a first aid kit and learn how to use it. A **survival bag** or thermal blanket could be useful if you're very cold.

water

survival bag

first aid kit

spare head torch

food

pocket knife

EXTREME BUT TRUE Big caving expeditions can take years to plan. They may be long trips, too—in one recent Russian exploration, a caver was underground for 24 days.

EMERGENCY!

Even the best-planned trip can go wrong. You could lose your way, become trapped by a flood, slip into a river, or be injured by a rock fall. So what should you do in an emergency?

Don't panic

Try to keep a clear head. Think before you act and don't make a bad situation worse. If you're lost, keep calm and try to retrace your steps, or work out where you are by studying a map. If a passage is blocked, look for an alternative route.

A rescue team straps an injured caver to a stretcher before carrying them out.

Don't disturb loose or crumbling rock: one falling stone may dislodge others and cause a cave collapse.

Stay safe

In a rock fall or flood, try to move into a safer area. Keep as dry and warm as possible—**hypothermia** is a serious risk underground. Stick with your friends and help each other. A cave rescue team may be able to reach you.

EXTREME BUT TRUE Don't forget that animals such as bears may live in caves! Check for signs of animal life, such as tracks or droppings, before entering any cave.

GLOSSARY

carabiner
An oval metal ring used to join two things together, such as a rope and harness.

chasm
A deep crack or split in rock.

claustrophobic
Suffering from claustrophobia, which is an extreme fear of small, cramped spaces.

current
Water moving in a certain direction. A strong current can sweep you off your feet, even if the water isn't deep!

glacier
A river of ice that forms over thousands of years, flowing very slowly down the side of a mountain.

glacier

hypothermia
A very dangerous condition in which a person becomes so cold that the body stops working properly. Without medical help, they may die.

limestone
A type of rock made over millions of years from the minerals and bones of tiny sea creatures lying on the seabed.

mineral
A solid substance that is produced naturally and made up of a mix of chemicals. Minerals may look like crystals, sand, or stone.

rappel
To slide down a rope using a harness and a device that allows you to control your speed and stop.

shaft
A deep, narrow, vertical hole that is often an entrance to a cave or mine.

stalactite
An icicle-shaped mass of solid mineral deposits, formed by dripping water, that hangs from the roof of a cave.

stalagmite
A mound or column of solid mineral deposits, formed by dripping water, that builds up on the floor of a cave.

As stalagmites and stalactites grow, they often join together.

survival bag
A large bag made of plastic or metal foil, used in emergencies by cavers and climbers to provide warmth and shelter.

stalagmite

WEBSITES

www.caves.org
Learn more about caving skills and equipment, and find caving clubs in your area.

www.cavingintro.net
Read great cave facts as well as important information about cave safety.

www.caverntours.com/KIDSPAGE_Formations.html
Look at amazing cave formations and discover how they are made.

INDEX

animals 11, 21
arches 6

carabiners 18, 22
cave diving 8, 16
cave grades 14, 15, 18
cave pearls 7
chimneys 15
climbing 5, 10, 12, 13, 15, 18
clothes 8, 9, 18
crawling 5, 9, 15
crystals 7

emergencies 20, 21

first aid kit 19
floods 5, 19, 20, 21
flowstones 7
footwear 9

gear 8, 9, 10, 11, 15, 18, 19
glaciers 6, 22
gloves 9

harnesses 10, 11
helmets 9, 11, 14
hypothermia 21, 22

knots 11

lakes 6, 16
lamps 4, 9, 13, 14, 16, 19
landslides 5
limestone 6, 22

minerals 7, 22

rappeling 5, 10, 11, 12, 13, 23
rescue teams 20, 21
rivers 6, 16, 18, 20
rock falls 9, 17, 20, 21
ropes 10, 11, 18

squeezes 15
stalactites 7, 23
stalagmites 7, 23
supplies 19
survival bags 19, 23
swimming 5, 8, 16

tools 17

underwater caves 8, 16, 17

waterproof 8, 18
waves 6
weather 19